The Tickly Monster

Written by Andrea Doering
Illustrated by Sue King

BARRON'S

The Tickly Monster knows ...

you have tickly fingers
and tickly toes!

He tickles your tummy

and knows you will giggle....

Then he tickles some more

...and you start to wiggle!

He tickles your knees,
as soft as you please.

Then under your chin, to see you grin!

He tickles with feathers
and fingers and fan ...

Until you're laughing so hard,
as hard as you can!

Then he packs up his things
and hugs you real tight,

hears your prayers, and
turns out the light.

"Sleep well," he says,
"Sweet dreams, Sweet Pea."